JAN 2009

To our sons, Robin Debevoise Lester and James Robinson Lester • R.L. & H.L.

For my sister Kaoruko • M.I.

To my dear children, Alex, Adam, Jason, Joshua, Daina, and Dustin. Love, Dad. • B.R.

Candlewick Press would like to extend special thanks to Bruce Raiffe, president of Gund, and all the staff at Gund for their help and cooperation.

Text copyright © 1995 by Robin and Helen Lester
Illustrations copyright © 1995 by Miko Imai
Based on the original character ™WUZZY copyright © 1985 by Gund Inc.

First edition 1995

Library of Congress Cataloging-in-Publication Data

Lester, Robin, 1939-
Wuzzy takes off / Robin & Helen Lester ; illustrated by Miko Imai.—1st ed.
(Gund children's library)
Summary: Wuzzy, a real live teddy bear who has always lived in the
woods, makes what he thinks is a trip to the moon and ends up at a
nearby playground.
ISBN 1-56402-498-9
[1. Teddy bears—Fiction. 2. Moon—Fiction.]
I. Lester, Helen. II. Imai, Miko, 1963—   ill. III. Title. IV. Series.
PZ7.L5634Wu   1995
[E]—dc20   95-10694

10 9 8 7 6 5 4 3 2 1

Printed in Hong Kong

The pictures in this book were done in watercolor and pencil.

Candlewick Press
2067 Massachusetts Avenue
Cambridge, Massachusetts 02140

WUZZY
TAKES OFF

Robin & Helen Lester   illustrated by Miko Imai

CANDLEWICK PRESS
CAMBRIDGE, MASSACHUSETTS

Wuzzy was the
snappiest dresser in the forest.
In fact, he was the only dresser
in the forest.

But as fancy as Wuzzy looked,
he was a woodsy bear who
lived his whole life among
the trees and rivers.

With his friends, Spike and
Frizzle, he played hide-and-seek,
climb-to-the-top-of-the-tree,
and hit-the-rock-with-the-log.

Wuzzy enjoyed these games,
but deep down he longed for
GREATER ADVENTURES.

One evening as the three friends were sitting by the river gazing at the moon, Wuzzy announced, "I'm going there tomorrow."

"Wow! The moon!" said Spike.

"How?" asked Frizzle.

"In a space capsule, of course."

"Of course," Spike and Frizzle nodded, looking puzzled.

The next morning, they went to see
Wuzzy off and found him already singing
in his space capsule.

"Yo dee ho, I'm taking off soon.

Ho dee yo, I'm bound for the moon."

Wuzzy swayed as he sang. He swayed so
hard that the capsule tipped over on its side
and began to roll. "I'm on my way!" he
called, as the capsule sped down the hill.

"Oh, dear," said Spike and Frizzle.

After what seemed like a
very long time, the capsule
came to a sudden stop. Wuzzy,
feeling a little woozy, wobbled
out and looked around. "What
a strange place—I must be on
the moon!" he shouted.

"I'm really, really, really on
the moon!"
Surprised that there were
deserts on the moon, he shook
the sand from his paws and
trotted off to explore.

He passed an oddly shaped river and came upon
a moon tree. "How can anyone play hide-and-seek
in branches like that?" Wuzzy wondered.

On he went until he came to another moon
tree, which had fallen across his path.

"Now, that looks like a perfect climber!"
he exclaimed. Wuzzy climbed

up **WOW!** and down very fast,

up **WOO!** and down very fast,

up **WHOA!** and down very fast.

He was just wondering how on earth
moon beings climbed to the tops of their
trees when — "Moon beings!" he gasped.

Wuzzy was a brave bear, but the creatures
coming toward him were not like anything
he'd ever seen. Their ears were stuck on
the sides of their heads, their paws were
oddly shaped, and some even had missing
fangs. Like bears, they came in various
shapes, sizes, and colors, but they had the
strangest fur—it was only
on their tops!

"So," thought Wuzzy, "Fuzzyheads
live on the moon."

The Fuzzyheads came toward
him—bouncing and skipping.
One was even rolling along
on its hind paws.

Wuzzy shivered as they came closer
and closer and closer. Then, to his
surprise, they picked him up gently
and passed him around. "Look!" they
cried. "A real live Teddy!"

Wuzzy was puzzled, for as far as he
knew, he was a real live Wuzzy. But
after they gave him some soft hugs and
pats, he decided that the Fuzzyheads
were not as scary as they looked.

Carefully they set him
down and began to play a
game. It was almost exactly
like hit-the-rock-with-a-log.
Wuzzy simply had to join in.

After he'd won the game with a home run, he rested on the grass with the Fuzzyheads. They must have liked him a lot, because they gave him what looked like a bag of moon rocks and said, "You'll love these — they're delicious."

"Odd that they would eat rocks," thought Wuzzy. He'd save his for later.

Suddenly a voice called, "Supper!"
and in an instant the Fuzzyheads were
gone. Could this be a magic moon word?

Wuzzy waited for his new friends,
hoping they would come back to play
more games. Maybe tomorrow.

It was growing dark, and he had begun
to miss Spike and Frizzle.

Back he trotted to his capsule and
dragged it through the moon dust to
a nearby hill.

"Yo dee ho, I'm going home soon.

Ho dee yo, I've been to the moon."

Wuzzy took off with dizzying
speed. When the capsule landed, a
woozy Wuzzy wobbled out, cheering
"Hooray! I'm back!"

The three friends sat by the river in the moonlight and Wuzzy told of the Fuzzyheads and of all the wonders he had seen. Then he shared his strawberry, orange, and chocolate moon rocks, which didn't last long.

That night, Wuzzy went to sleep with moon rock juice on his fuzzy face and dreamed of more adventures to come.